THE HUNT FOR
HAN SOLO

#5
THE HUNT FOR
HAN SOLO

DAVE WOLVERTON

SCHOLASTIC INC.
New York   Toronto   London   Auckland   Sydney

No part of this publication may be reproduced in whole or in part, or stored in a retrieval system, or transmitted in any form or by any means, electronic, mechanical, photocopying, recording, or otherwise, without written permission of the publisher. For information regarding permission, write to Scholastic Inc., Attention: Permissions Department, 555 Broadway, New York, NY 10012.

ISBN 0-590-12797-7

™ & ® & © 1998 by Lucasfilm Ltd.
All rights reserved. Published by Scholastic Inc. Used Under Authorization.

SCHOLASTIC and associated logos are trademarks and/or
registered trademarks of Scholastic Inc.

12 11 10 9 8 7 6 5 4 3 2   8 9/9 0 1 2/0

Printed in the U.S.A.

First Scholastic printing, January 1998

THE HUNT FOR HAN SOLO

PRELIMINARY MISSION

CHAPTER ONE

Han Solo had hoped there would be one corner of the galaxy to hide in after he helped Luke Skywalker blow up the Death Star. There wasn't.

The planet Faldos was on the far edge of the galaxy, a dirty little backwater planet used only by a few smugglers. Stolen weapons, armor, and technology were sold there. Guns for the Rebellion or the underworld — whoever paid highest. Han Solo thought he'd be safe.

No such luck.

Now he was cornered, alongside Luke Skywalker, Princess Leia, and his trusted copilot Chewbacca. They were trapped in the hallway of a hotel, and the situation looked grim.

A blaster charge exploded near Solo's ear, and he wedged himself tighter against the wall at the top of the staircase. Luke, Leia, and Chewbacca were right behind him. A second bolt slammed into the far wall.

The Restful Nights Hotel was turning out to be anything but restful! Right now, three lobby attendants had Solo pinned at the top floor, while the desk manager called for backup.

"Give it up, Solo!" one of the lobby attendants shouted. "There's no way out!"

"Hey," Solo shouted, "what did I ever do to you?" He stuck his blaster around the corner and pulled the trigger, hoping to scare them off. There was a horrible scream as the blaster erupted. Someone had been trying to sneak up on him.

"All right," the desk manager shouted, "now you're in for it. That was my brother!"

"Sorry!" Solo said.

"That's not good enough — I want your head!" the manager bellowed. It seemed everyone wanted Solo's head nowadays. The Empire was after him, and so was the crime lord Jabba the Hutt. Though the criminal scum on this planet probably wouldn't turn Solo in to the Empire, they would be happy to collect a bounty from Jabba.

Solo glanced around the corner. The lobby attendants had taken cover behind the manager's desk. The manager was on the comlink, gesticulating wildly as he shouted. "Yeah," he said, *"Han Solo!* The one with the bounties on his head . . . here in the hotel!"

"Hold them off for a minute," Luke said. "I think I've almost got it!" Solo glanced behind him to see Luke furiously punching a lock pad, hoping to find the right code combination to open the door. *May the Force be with you*, Solo thought.

"Okay, hotshot," Leia told Han. "You promised us a nice room, and instead you're going to get us all killed!"

"It's not my fault!" Solo protested. "How was I supposed to know that the clerks here all want to be bounty hunters?"

"Looks like it's up to me," Leia said. She reached into a pocket of her coveralls and pulled out a detonation device. Quickly she punched the arming button and let it roll down the stairs.

In half a second there was a huge explosion, accompanied by the crash of shattering vases and splintering wood. Light and heat erupted up the stairwell.

Solo glanced down into the lobby, where several clerks poked their heads up from behind the check-in counter. Now they were *really* mad.

The manager shouted into his comlink, "Security, get in here, now!"

Several security goons rushed in from a back door — two huge aliens with four arms each, both wearing full armor and brandishing heavy blaster rifles.

"Hand me some more detonators!" Solo shouted to Leia. Just as he'd hoped, the words caused the desk manager and his goons to scurry for cover.

More quietly, he whispered to Chewbacca, "Chewie, give Luke a hand with one of those doors, would ya?"

Chewbacca roared, pushed Luke away from the door, then slammed his huge shoulder against it. The door burst inward, splintering to pieces.

As Solo dove in behind Chewie, he imagined that some poor family would be terrified by their abrupt entry. He had an apology ready as he rushed into the living room.

He couldn't believe what he found.

Two whiphid thugs were sitting on couches. A squirming sack was on the floor between them. Solo had seen enough slave traders to know a kidnapping when he saw one. His suspicions were confirmed when one of the thugs aimed a heavy blaster right between his eyes.

"Hold it right there!" the fellow growled. He was a big man, with a glittering blue cybernetic eye and a tattoo of a krayt dragon covering the left half of his face.

"Whatever you say, pal," Solo said, half raising his hands. He added, "By the way, you dropped a coin."

The thug looked down. In that instant, Solo clubbed him in the head with the butt of his blaster. The other kidnapper leaped off the couch to grab his fallen partner's weapon. Chewbacca thumped him from behind, sending the thug over the couch and into a wall. As he hit, bits of plaster fell from the ceiling.

Just then Leia and Luke rushed into the room. Solo grabbed the squirming sack and leaped through the nearest window, rolling to the ground some ten feet below. The others followed.

They sprinted down a street and around a corner. In the gunrunner's market, they were soon just part of the crowd.

As they hurried back to the spaceport, Solo could hear the hotel manager shouting, his voice shaking with rage, "You'll pay for this, Han Solo! Every damaged piece of furniture! You'll pay!"

When they reached the *Millennium Falcon*, the golden droid See-Threepio took one look at the squirming bag and chided, "Why Captain Solo, you haven't kidnapped someone, have you? I'm certain the authorities would not appreciate it if you have!"

"No, my rusting friend, I didn't kidnap anyone. I've *rescued* someone. It's an old habit of mine — one I'm trying to break. Now give me a minute to see if I can get us off this rock before whatever passes for security on this planet comes and blows the ship into scrap metal."

Solo and Chewbacca leaped to their seats and fired the

thrusters while Luke and Leia strapped themselves into their safety harnesses.

A moment later, the *Falcon* took off into space. Solo checked his scanners for signs of pursuit.

When he felt sure that no one was following him, Solo and Chewbacca carried the squirming bag back to the passenger bay. Luke, Leia, the droid Artoo-Detoo, and See-Threepio all gathered around. Solo opened the bag by pulling a string.

As the bag fell open, Solo saw something that both disgusted and intrigued him: Inside the bag was a brown creature, wormlike in appearance, with an enormous mouth and two cruel eyes that shone like gold.

"A baby Hutt?" Luke asked, unsure. Chewie roared and nodded.

The baby Hutt flowed across the ground like liquid, came to Solo, and gazed up at him from knee height. It could not have weighed much more than a bowling ball, but it seemed too long for its weight.

The creature gazed at Solo for half a second, then bit his knee.

"Ow!" Solo said, kicking at the little savage. "Is that the thanks I get for saving your worthless hide?"

"Ha, ha, ha," it laughed in a throaty growl. "I love the taste of fresh meat, human."

A baby Hutt.

"So, you little carrion eater," Solo said, "what do I call you?"

"Grubba," the youngster replied.

"Good," Solo said, smiling with false pleasure. "It's nice

to meet you, Grubba. So, tell me — there must be someone who is in charge of you. Someone who will be real happy to see you? Maybe happy enough to offer a big reward?"

The baby Hutt nodded enthusiastically and made a rude noise like a burp. "Jabba. My Ur-Damo is Jabba."

Solo tried to contain his surprise. He smiled broadly. Maybe, just maybe, if he gave Jabba the child, Jabba would take the bounty off Solo's head. "Grubba, my friend," Solo said, "you don't know what a pleasure it is to meet you!"

CHAPTER TWO

"Oh, this is a hideous world," the Prefect Eugene Talmont said with a sigh. He leaned on his gold-handled walking stick and gazed out his office window, overlooking the Mos Eisley spaceport. A huge storm had just blown through. Yellow dust hung heavy in the air. Tawny grime had settled onto buildings, speeders, banthas — everything. Even the little Jawas scurrying through the streets on their secretive errands wore dark robes coated in dust. Both of Tatooine's suns had just risen, and the heat beating in through the window felt like a blast furnace.

The Prefect Eugene Talmont was the Empire's chief administrator for this world. "There must be a way out of here," he muttered to his audience of bounty hunters. "My father was always assigned to decent posts, yet I am a far better man than he. It almost seems that the Empire is punishing me for my excellent skills."

True, Tatooine was a tough world to govern, full of ruffians and outlaws. The moisture farmers were too poor to tax, and the local criminals sometimes delighted in tearing Talmont's tax collectors and lawmen into little tiny pieces. The Empire never gave Talmont enough troops to properly subdue the planet. Talmont often comforted himself by saying it was an "opportunity" to tame the barbaric rock, but lately he had begun to wonder if perhaps someone higher up in the chain of command disliked him.

"Soon, with your help, I will be able to move to a better world." He turned to the bounty hunters gathered behind him in his office.

Among them, the most imposing was Dengar. He wasn't the largest of the bounty hunters, but the big man had a cold and impassive look; his head was swathed in bandages to hide old scars. Years ago, while racing the Rebel pawn Han Solo, Dengar had nearly been killed. Afterward, he gained a reputation as an Imperial assassin and bounty hunter. Now the man was eager to hunt Han Solo down — so eager that he had volunteered to blast Solo for free.

According to the papers on Prefect Talmont's desk, Solo had helped the Rebels destroy the Empire's greatest weapon, the Imperial Death Star, only a few weeks ago. The Empire had since put a fabulous bounty on Solo's head — dead or alive. Dengar wanted him dead.

Besides Dengar, there were two others in the group.

The first was a gray-skinned creature with a long snout, called a Kubaz, from the planet Kubindi. The Kubaz greatly admired social insects, and had a philosophy based on the concept of following their queen without question. This creature, named Udin, couldn't understand why Han Solo would fight his own Emperor. Udin carried a laser rifle slung over his shoulder, with which he planned to fry Han Solo and his insane Rebel cohorts.

Last was Eron Stonefield, a beautiful human woman who had only recently begun working as a freelance bounty hunter. Her long red hair flowed in gentle waves to the middle of her back, and her fair complexion remained pale despite the planet's perpetual sun. Talmont was unsure about her loyalties. She was a decent woman who disliked Tatooine as much as Talmont did, and hoped to use her share of the bounty to make a better life for herself. Like Talmont, she'd been born into the service of the Empire, and felt uneasy about much of what the Emperor was doing. Talmont felt she was on the verge of becoming a Rebel herself. But Solo's reputation as a criminal in the service of Jabba the Hutt kept Eron from sympathizing with the man. And as an expert in martial arts, she was as deadly as she was talented.

"So, you all know why we are gathered," Prefect Talmont continued. "Solo is evasive and dangerous. But he has yet to deal with me!"

"Excuse me, oh great Lord of Tatooine," Udin the Kubaz said with a gentle wiggle of his snout. An electronic interpreting device slung around his neck spoke in an unnaturally pleasant voice, "I am but a simple hunter, and do not understand your brilliant plan. You say that we will stalk Han Solo here on Tatooine. But why should he come here? Doesn't Jabba, the most imperious of Hutts, have a bounty on Han Solo? My simple mind has me thinking that Han Solo will avoid this place more than all others."

Udin nodded his head as he spoke, showing his servitude to the great leader Talmont.

"Explain it to him," Talmont said, waving his hand to Eron. "You've been following this case."

Eron Stonefield nodded. She spoke in a firm voice. "As we all know, Han Solo helped destroy the Death Star. This treason has landed him on the Empire's list of most-wanted villains. The Empire will pay handsomely for Solo. But Jabba also wants him.

"Solo must hide from the Empire. With the crime lords hunting for him, he cannot continue to hide in the underworld. So he must pay off Jabba if he wants to live.

"I don't think we need to hunt Solo. I've been expecting

him to come here. I've spent considerable efforts trying to decode all incoming transmissions. In the next few days, Solo will likely come to Tatooine to pay off Jabba. But we will be waiting for him. Once we nab him, we'll have the money he plans to use to pay off Jabba. Jabba will then pay us his bounty, and the Empire will pay us the reward. Between the three payoffs, this should make us rich."

"And don't forget," Eugene Talmont added, "I will be paying you, too.

"Our plan is simple," Talmont continued. "Jabba the Hutt lives in an ancient fortress on the edge of the Dune Sea, across the Jundland Wastes. You will camp there with monitoring equipment and vehicles. When Han Solo flies to Jabba's fortress, you will apprehend him. You will get your reward, and I will get sent to a post on a far, far better world. You have my word on that. My solemn word."

CHAPTER THREE

At the Mos Eisley spaceport, the bounty hunters soon prepared their vehicles. The deserts of Tatooine were treacherous, and the sand from a storm could quickly destroy most engines. In light of this, Udin the Kubaz decided to ride a bantha into the desert. Eron Stonefield elected to ride a dewback, for though the creature was slow, it could stand the blistering heat of Tatooine's two suns. Dengar, however, trusted his personal speeder bike more than some bantha or lizard. The speeder was faster than the animals, and if Dengar had to chase Solo down, he would need a fast vehicle.

Udin hooked a large wagon to his bantha — a wagon filled with active sensors that would detect any ship that tried to land near Jabba's palace. The wagon also contained communications gear, weapons, food, and camping equipment — the bounty hunters tried to prepare for any situation, no matter how life-threatening. Chief among this equipment was an inflatable biosphere, a dome for the bounty hunters to live in out in the desert. The dome stayed cool in the hot sun, and its spun carbon filaments were tough enough to withstand any sandstorm.

After checking over their survival gear, the bounty hunters were off into the Wastes.

The Jundland Wastes were filled with rocky hills and crags of old lava rocks, with valleys worn smooth by wind and sand. The area was said to be the home of any number of beasts. Jawas scavenged the Wastes, as did the Sand

People. But rumor said that even worse creatures lived among the rocks — dune worms and krayt dragons.

As Dengar rode beside the dewback and bantha, Eron Stonefield smiled down at him. Perhaps because they were both human, she felt some connection to him. Dengar didn't share her feeling. After he'd wrecked his speeder bike in the race on Corellia, the Empire had saved him — for a price. In order to make him a better assassin for the Empire, the Imperial surgeons had cut out the part of his brain that let him feel human compassion.

"What are you thinking?" Eron asked. "You were smiling."

Dengar wondered at that. He'd been imagining Han Solo trying to dodge as he pulled the trigger of his blaster. He'd smiled at the thought of revenge against Solo.

"I was thinking about what a pleasure it will be to meet Han Solo again."

"You want to fight him? He won't be alone, you know. He has his Wookiee friend."

Dengar nodded. "His fuzzy friend won't save him this time."

On the bantha, Udin leaned forward. Large stinging flies were crawling all over his mount, and Udin sucked several of them up. "This is not a good world," he said. "The insects here are dry and flavorless."

Just then something caught his eye. On the bantha, he was up higher than the others. Squinting, he peered over a rocky crag. "Trouble ahead," his electronic translator buzzed. "Creatures on banthas. They have blasters."

Eron stopped her dewback, then jumped onto a rock pile and climbed up to look over. "Sand People," she said.

"About a dozen of them on the trail up ahead. They look like they're setting an ambush. You see over there — at least one of them is pointing toward a possible spot to hide."

Eron aimed her heavy blaster rifle and fired. Her shot was high and to the right, but it hit the cliff above the Sand People and sent small rocks tumbling onto the foremost bantha and rider. The Sand People quickly turned their animals in the narrow canyon and sped away.

"They're gone," she said. "For the moment. But if I know Sand People, they'll be back on our trail soon."

"Why would they want us?" Udin asked. "We have only a few bugs to eat, and none of them are very tasty."

"They want our bodies," Eron answered. "They'll drain the water from us and throw the rest away."

"We could hunt them down," Dengar said. "Neutralize them before they warn their friends."

"No," Eron said. "It would be dangerous to chase them through these canyons. Besides, we don't need to chase them. Given time, they'll come to us. . . . "

For the next two days the bounty hunters traveled, making their best time at night, sleeping in the narrow canyons during the heat of the day.

They left the Jundland Wastes, and traveled faster on the edge of the Dune Sea. By the third night, they set camp on a small outcropping of rock near Jabba's palace.

Dengar and Udin installed the sensor dishes. In the quiet of the night, Dengar stood for a long time looking up at falling stars, wondering if one of the flashes might be Han Solo, dropping out of hyperspace.

* * *

On board the *Millennium Falcon*, Leia looked out the view screen to the planet Tatooine below.

"I hope you know what you're doing," she told Solo. "I get the feeling this is a trap."

"What do you mean?" Solo asked. "Jabba will be thrilled that I rescued his Ur-Damin." Over the past few days, Solo and the others had learned that young Grubba was not Jabba's child. Instead, Grubba was the offspring of one of his siblings. The title Ur-Damin meant that Grubba was something of a favored nephew or niece, while the title Ur-Damo referred to an illustrious uncle or aunt. Young Grubba had been on the way to Jabba's palace, where he was to begin learning the finer points of running a criminal organization. It was a great honor for young Grubba to be brought into the family business this way, and for Jabba to be the young Hutt's tutor. However, Grubba had been kidnapped before he reached Tatooine. Solo knew that the ties between the Hutts were strong. Family honor would no doubt dictate that Jabba save the child at any cost.

"You know what I mean," Leia said. "Jabba doesn't know who kidnapped Grubba, and I don't think he's going to believe that you just happened to break into a room and 'save' the child from kidnappers."

"But that's how it happened!" Solo objected.

Leia shook her head. They were discussing this in private — Luke and the others were all in the berthing quarters. Leia sat down in the copilot's seat with a sigh. "Look, Jabba would have to be a fool to believe such a story. And even if he *did* believe you, why should he let you go? He'll swap for Grubba, and he might even offer to remove the bounty he's offered for your head. But you won't get far before his men turn on you. There's still the Imperial reward."

"Trust me, princess," Solo said, "Jabba won't try to collect any Imperial reward. Aside from bribing a few officials, he dislikes the Empire as much as I do."

"You only believe you're safe because you want to believe it," Leia said.

"I don't *want* to believe it. I *have* to believe it," Solo declared. "I don't have a choice."

On the edge of the Dune Sea, Udin and the others sat in the biosphere and listened to the wind howl. Dawn had come an hour ago, and as often happened on the Dune Sea, the cool night winds gave way to severe storms. Udin poked his head out and saw a huge twister in the distance, rising up hundreds of feet.

The sensor console beeped a warning and Udin turned to the monitor. There was no way to know whether the sensors were really picking up an incoming ship, since the sensor waves could be detecting a dust cloud or ionized gas from the storm. He swatted the machinery once for good measure and watched the incoming craft. It moved in a perfectly straight line, against the wind. A dust cloud would have blown *with* the wind.

"My esteemed colleagues," Udin said with a scrunching of his trunk. "A ship is coming in."

"Another one?" Dengar asked.

A dozen ships had landed in the past couple of days. If

the authorities on Tatooine had recognized the breadth of Jabba's smuggling operation, perhaps someone would have tried harder to shut it down.

"Indeed. But this one is not landing so close to the palace," Udin offered.

"Let me take a look," Eron said. She leaned over Udin's shoulder, studying the monitor. "Whoever it is, they're coming in close, but not too close."

Eron stared out at the violent churn of the storm. It was a small miracle that the biosphere remained intact — everything else appeared to fall to the mercy of the incredible blasts of sand and wind.

"In this sandstorm," Dengar said, "only an extremely confident pilot would try to land close to a large building."

"This could be Solo's ship," Eron said. "We should definitely send someone to check it out."

No one wanted to go out in that storm. The sand blowing off the Dune Sea could cut flesh to ribbons.

But someone had to go.

MISSION BRIEFING

Before you proceed, you must consult the Mission Guide for the rules of the STAR WARS MISSIONS. You must follow these rules at all times.

This is a Bounty Hunter/Imperial Mission.

You have been hired to track down Han Solo and his Rebel allies on the planet Tatooine. You and your fellow bounty hunters are hidden in the desert outside Jabba's palace. Your sensors tell you that during a severe sandstorm, a ship has landed near Jabba's palace. You must go out into the storm and verify that this is Solo's ship. If it is, you are to report to the others via communicator. Then you are to capture Solo, preferably alive.

In addition to your weapon and your communicator, you carry a locator that sends a signal to your fellow bounty hunters, so they can guide you toward your target.

You start the Mission with your MP total from your previous Mission. (Or 1,000 MP, if this is your first Mission.)

Choose your character now.

You can take two weapons of your choice. Choose wisely — the Dune Sea is a dangerous place.

For a vehicle, you must ride the dewback. The giant lizards move at a plodding pace, but are accustomed to the fierce desert storms. The speeder is worthless in this weather.

You can use Power twice on this Mission.

Good luck.

Your Mission:
The Hunt for
Han Solo

You gather your weapons and prepare to go into the sandstorm. To protect your eyes, you wear goggles. You also place a rag over your mouth and a battle helmet over your head. Protective clothing covers most of your body.

You adjust your communicator to the proper frequency so that you can report back to the others and receive assistance. Once you are ready, you open the door of the biosphere.

Immediately, stinging sand blows into the biosphere. You fight your way out into the storm. Even with your goggles, you cannot see far ahead.

Both the bantha and the dewback have put their heads against a large rock, so their bodies shield their heads from the wind. Their eyes are closed.

You saddle the dewback, climb on, and kick the beast sharply. It opens its eyes to mere slits, and seems angry when you command it to head into the storm. But once it gets moving, the dewback seems eager to end its journey and withdraw out of the weather, so it moves along at a reasonable pace.

You flip on the communicator. "Base, can you hear me?" you ask.

The communicator is fit with a scrambler, so that outsiders can't decode your transmission. The scrambler alters the voice of the speaker, so that you can't tell who answers. "Yes," a voice replies. "Your locator beacon signal is coming in strong. Head due west, until I tell you otherwise."

You can tell by the shape of a nearby dune that you are heading roughly northwest, and you urge the dewback to turn. But now the dewback is walking almost directly into the wind. If it heads northwest, the wind won't hit its face.

It walks a few paces and turns a bit, hoping to fool you. You urge it back in the direction you want to go, but a moment later the lizard turns again.

To steer the dewback on course, you may use persuasion without Power, persuasion with Power, or physical force.

To persuade the dewback (without Power): You whisper words of encouragement to the creature while keeping a firm grip on the reins. Your charm# +2 is your confront#. Roll the 6-dice to persuade the dewback.

> If your confront# is equal to or more than your roll number, add 4 MP to your MP total. You have a gift for handling this dewback, and it will follow you anywhere.

> If your confront# is lower than your roll#, subtract the difference from your MP total. The stubborn animal doesn't like you. It lopes off course, and you must use physical force to turn it (below).

To persuade the dewback (using Power)*: You must use your Persuasion Power. Your charm# + your Power# + your Power's low-resist# is your confront#. Roll the 6-dice.

> If your confront# is equal to or more than your roll number, add the difference to your MP total. The dewback is firmly under your influence.

> If your confront# is lower than your roll#, subtract the difference from your MP total. The dewback begins lop-

ing off course, and you must use physical force to get it back under control (below).

Note: This counts as one of two Power uses you are allowed on this Mission.

To turn the dewback using physical force: Your strength# +1 is your confront#. Roll the 6-dice to turn the dewback.

If your confront# is equal to or more than your roll#, add the difference to your MP total. The dewback is under your command, and you may proceed.

If your confront# is lower than your roll#, subtract the difference from your MP total and repeat this confront until you have subdued the dewback.

You keep heading west as the storm grows stronger. Wind whips past your face and batters you. Your eye goggles are getting scratched by the fierce sand.

Worse, the dust clouds are now so high that they block the sun. It's dark as night. You can't recognize any landmarks, so you grit your teeth and bear it.

You travel like this for an hour, and twice you get messages on your communicator telling you to turn to your left. Each time you get a message, it is fainter than the last. The sandstorm is interfering with your signal.

Suddenly you see something large and solid-looking ahead. Perhaps, you think, it is a rock that will give you some shelter from the wind.

But seconds later, you recognize that it is not a rock at

all: Two Sand People are riding toward you on a bantha! Behind them is another bantha, and another.

Involuntarily, you cry out in surprise.

The Sand Person in front points at you excitedly and shouts, raising its gaffi stick in the air. The one behind it fumbles to pull a long rifle from a holster. Even the bantha seems to recognize that you are an enemy. It lowers its massive horns and stamps the ground, preparing to charge.

On the communicator, your friends cry out, "What's wrong?"

You must choose to evade or combat the charging bantha.

To evade the bantha (without Power): Your stealth# +1 is your confront#. Roll the 6-dice to evade the bantha.

If your confront# is equal to or more than your roll#, add the difference +3 to your MP total. You lose the bantha and the Sand People in the storm and may now proceed.

If your confront# is lower than your roll#, subtract the difference from your MP total. The bantha is charging and you must combat it (below).

To evade the bantha (using Power)*: Choose your Evasion Power. Your stealth# + your Power's mid-resist# + your Power# is your confront#. Roll the 6-dice to slip past the creature.

If your confront# is equal to or more than your roll#, add the difference +3 to your MP total. You lose the bantha and the Sand People in the storm. You may now proceed.

If your confront# is lower than your roll#, subtract the difference from your MP total. The bantha is charging and you must combat it (below).

*Note: This counts as one of two Power uses you are allowed on this Mission.

To combat the charging bantha: Choose your weapon. Add your weaponry# to your weapon's mid-range# +3 for your confront number. Roll the 12-dice to shoot the bantha.

If your confront# is equal to or more than your roll#, add the difference to your MP total. It's a perfect hit — now you must face the Sand People (below).

If your confront# is lower than your roll#, subtract the difference from your MP total. Add +2 to your confront# for your new confront#.

If your new confront# is equal to or more than your roll#, it's a perfect hit. Now you must face the Sand People (below).

If your new confront# is lower than your roll#, subtract the difference from your MP total and repeat this confront until you have felled the bantha. You must then face the Sand People (below).

To face the Sand People: The charging bantha goes down. The Sand Person in front rolls to his feet and charges, shouting a battle cry. He is waving his gaffi stick threateningly. Another Sand Person seems to have been knocked unconscious by the fall. Behind them, the other Sand People are so surprised that they turn their mounts in all directions and run. (In the blinding sandstorm, you cannot see where they go.) The remaining Sand Person rushes up to you and swings his gaffi stick, seeking to disarm you. You must defend yourself.

To defend yourself: Add your strength# to your skill# for your confront#. Roll the 6-dice.

> *If your confront# is equal to or more than your roll#,* the Sand Person misses his attack, and you must choose to combat him with your weapon or hand-to-hand.

> *If your confront# is lower than your roll#,* your weapon goes flying off, and you must fight him hand-to-hand.

To combat the Sand Person hand-to-hand: Add your strength# to your skill# +4 for your confront#. Roll the 12-dice to knock down the Sand Person.

> *If your confront# is equal to or more than your roll#,* add the difference to your MP total. The Sand Person is out of commission. You may proceed.

> *If your confront# is lower than your roll#,* subtract the difference from your MP total. Add +1 to your confront# for your new confront#. Repeat this confront using the new confront# until you have defeated the Sand Person.

To combat the Sand Person with your weapon: Choose your weapon. Add your weaponry# to your weapon's close-range# for your confront#. Roll the 6-dice to combat the Sand Person.

If your confront# is equal to or more than your roll#, add the difference to your MP total. The Sand Person won't bother you again. You may proceed.

If your confront# is less than your roll#, subtract the difference from your MP total and repeat this confront until you have defeated the Sand Person.

Once you have defeated or evaded the bantha and the Sand Person, add 25 MP to your MP total (40 MP for Advanced Level players). If you defeated the Sand Person in combat, you can take his gaffi stick.

Whew, that was close!

You continue on your way. Every few minutes, you get directions from your comrades over the communicator, telling you which way to turn.

But the interference on your communicator becomes so heavy that at last you find yourself shouting, "Which way? Which way do I go?"

"Strai . . . *crackle, crackle* . . . ed. You're almost . . . *crackle crackle.*" the tinny voice answers. And then you hear nothing but static.

Relentlessly you press forward. In the darkness ahead, a building suddenly appears. It's a great fortress made of black plascrete, and it is very, very old. Such plascrete is often used as armor plating on military ships, but these battlements have been worn and pitted until little is left. You have heard that Jabba's palace is built in an ancient fortress built by the B'omarr monks. This smaller fortress looks as if it was once some kind of B'omarr outpost.

Still, there must be some kind of courtyard within the walls. Han Solo might well have set his ship down within the safety of this fortress.

The thought excites you. Only a fine pilot like Solo could manage to set a ship down inside these walls during a storm.

You watch the tops of the battlements for guards, but see none. You ride around the building, searching for a way in, and find a huge gate that has been left half open.

Through clouds of swirling sand, you see what might be the dim landing lights of a ship. You take your dewback to the rear of the building to hide it where it will be shielded from the wind.

Sand has blown against the wall, and has built up in a high drift. You realize that if you stand on the dewback, you could jump up to the wall and scurry over, then sneak into the fortress.

Knowing that you might come face-to-face with Han Solo or his Wookiee friend at any moment, you draw your weapon.

You must climb over the wall.

To climb over the wall: Add your strength# to your skill# +3 for your confront#. Roll the 12-dice to climb the wall.

If your confront# is equal to or more than your roll#, add the difference +5 to your MP total. You find a handhold in the crumbling fortress and pull yourself to the top of the wall. You may proceed.

If your confront# is lower than your roll#, subtract the difference from your MP total. Add +2 to your confront# for your new confront#.

> *If your new confront# is equal to or more than your roll#, you pull yourself over the wall and may proceed.*

> *If your new confront# is lower than your roll#, subtract the difference from your MP total and repeat this confront until you have climbed over the wall.*

You climb onto a walkway atop the wall and look down the other side. The outpost is much larger than you had imagined. Most of it is covered by mounds of sand, but you see a ship within a cleared courtyard a few hundred yards away. The lights from its landing bay are shining, and even as you watch, you see two shadowy figures enter the ship.

It might be Solo! He could be getting away!

You check the walkway atop the wall. You duck low and run toward the nearest tower. From there you hope to find some stairs that will take you down closer to the ship.

As you enter the tower, you find yourself in an alcove, looking down into an ancient amphitheater. There are stained-glass windows above you, and the dim light shining from above lets you see grim scenes.

In one scene, a person in yellow robes is kneeling so that his head is lying on a sacrificial altar. A second person stands above him with a laser scalpel that shines like a dim silver lightsaber.

In a second picture, the person who was lying on the altar is dead. His skull has been opened, and the second person holds the dead man's brain high in the air.

In a third picture, the brain itself floats among the bright stars of the galaxy, light shining from it as if it is a burning sun.

You get a *very* creepy feeling about this place.

The chapel below has an altar in the center, with theater seats rising up all around it. You need to get down to that lower level.

But in the far corner of the chapel, along the walkway at your level, something large and dark scurries past the far door. It looks like a giant spider, as big as you!

You lower yourself from the walkway and drop down to the back seats of the ancient amphitheater, then walk down the stone steps to where the altar sits.

There must be a door nearby. You hope. . . .

You stand near the altar. There are seats behind you, and ahead is a semicircle that may have once held viewing seats above and around the altar. But no seats remain, only a dozen large holes, each about half the height of a man. They look like service tunnels.

You search for another door, but the back of the chapel is in complete shadow. If there's a door back there, you can't see it.

You hear a scraping sound above you and look above the altar. A large spiderlike droid issues from one of the service tunnels. You know it is a droid because of the red running lights shining beneath its metal body. The droid sits ominously silent.

"Greetings, devoted one," a voice says. You look up and notice an old rusted speaker above the altar, along with a camera. Someone is watching you from another room. You don't know where this person might be. "Lay your head upon the altar, and we shall free you from this earthly realm. A monk shall be here soon to perform the surgery, but the droid will help you prepare."

The droid raises a laser scalpel and flips it on. A flickering stream of light issues from it.

You gulp. "Uh, not today, thank you." You step back and look up. Above you, another spider droid is blocking the door you entered. It, too, carries a laser scalpel.

As it comes through the doorway, the doors behind it slide closed with a hiss. The room is suddenly dark, except for the dim light shining through the stained-glass windows, and the evil red running lights of the droids themselves.

The spider droid stares at you with dull electronic eyes. Behind you, you hear the scrabbling of metal legs scraping stone. Echoing from some dark passage, you hear a mad giggling noise. The monk is coming!

To escape, you must either lie to the speaker or fight the droids.

To lie (without Power): You say that you represent Sorosuub Computerized Home Maintenance Corporation, and you only stopped here to seek shelter from the storm. You remind them that Sorosuub is able to handle all of their maintenance needs. Your charm# +1 is your confront#. Roll the 6-dice to deceive the speaker.

If your confront # is equal to or more than your roll number, add 10 MP to your MP total. The voice tells you that his entertainment system has been broken for a very long time. He can no longer pick up the ballet and musicals from Mos Eisley. He asks you to go downstairs. This makes you nervous, because you know that you will be in the presence of the monks.

If your confront# is lower than your roll#, subtract the difference from your MP total. The voice doesn't believe you. He orders the droids to restrain you. You must combat them (below).

To lie (using Power)*: Choose your Persuasion or Deception Power. Your stealth# + your Power# + your Power's low-resist# is your confront#. You say that you are a specialist in home repairs for Sorosuub, and you only stopped here seeking shelter from the storm. Roll the 6-dice to deceive the voice.

If your confront# is equal to or more than your roll#, add 10 MP to your MP total. The voice tells you that his entertainment system has been broken for a very long time. He can no longer pick up the ballet and musicals from Mos Eisley. He asks you to go downstairs. This makes you nervous, because you know that you will be in the presence of the monks.

If your confront# is lower than your roll#, subtract the difference from your MP total. The voice doesn't believe you, and orders the droids to restrain you. You must combat the droids (below).

*Note: This counts as one of two Power uses you are allowed on this Mission.

To combat the droids (one at a time): Add your weaponry# +1 to your weapon's close-range# for your confront#. Roll the 6-dice to combat the first droid.

If your confront# is equal to or more than your roll#, add the difference to your MP total, and proceed to combat the second droid, and then the third, using the same confront equation.

If your confront# is lower than your roll#, subtract the difference from your MP total and repeat this confront. Once you defeat the first droid, repeat this confront to battle the second droid, and then the third, using the same confront equation.

Once you have defeated all the droids, add 30MP to your total. (50MP for Advanced Level players). If you fought the droids, you may add a laser scalpel to your personal arsenal.

At the back of the room, you find a doorway. You head down into the depths, following a winding stairwell that goes deep into the earth.

Soon the stone walls become dark and damp, and the air feels cool and moist. You realize that by Tatooine's standards, there must be a fortune's worth of water in this air.

When you reach the bottom of the stairs, you find a locked door. The locking mechanism is old and rusted together. You want to open it silently, in case there are more droids around.

You can either use Power to open the lock, use your laser scalpel to open the lock, or force it open physically.

To open the lock (using Power)*: Choose your Object Movement Power. Your skill# + your Power's low-resist# + your Power# is your confront#. Roll the 6-dice to open the lock.

If your confront# is equal to or more than your roll#, add the difference to your MP total. The door swings open easily. You may now proceed.

If your confront# is lower than your roll#, subtract the difference from your MP total. Repeat this confront until you have opened the door, and then proceed.

*Note: This counts as one of two Power uses you are allowed on this Mission.

To open the lock using the laser scalpel, add your weaponry# to your weapon's short-range# for your confront#. Roll a 6-dice to open the door silently.

If your confront# is equal to or more than your roll#, add the difference to your MP total. The door silently swings open.

If your confront# is lower than your roll#, subtract the difference from your MP total. Repeat this confront using the same confront# until you have opened the door, and then proceed.

To open the door with physical force: Your strength# +3 is your confront#. Roll the 6-dice to open the door.

If your confront# is equal to or more than your roll#, add the difference to your MP total. The door swings open.

If your confront# is lower than your roll#, subtract the difference from your MP total. Repeat this confront using the same confront# until you have opened the door.

A grisly sight awaits you.

The door opens onto a vast room filled with dozens of spider droids, overturned on tables like dead bugs. These droids are in need of repair, and some have been robbed of spare parts.

Beyond the droids you see something even more disturbing: Along one wall is a shelf, and on it are glowing jars, lit from beneath. Within each jar is a brain, floating in a greenish liquid. Some jars are dim, no longer functioning. The brains within these jars are brown and dry.

A huge vat of green nutrient solution is pumped through clear pipes to each brain, from a container at the bottom of the far wall.

Not all of the brains are human. You see some alien brains, with neural webs that look like root systems. Some of these brains are quite small, which doesn't surprise you, since you quickly deduce that only a pinhead would allow some monk to remove his brain — if he had a choice.

However, one of the brains must be from some very

large creature, for it is floating in a huge container the size of a large barrel. The other still-living brains are clustered around it, like planets circling a sun. You wonder what kind of monster such a brain would have come from.

"Greetings, oh bounty hunter," the largest brain says.

"Greetings to you, oh floating brain," you answer. Suddenly, you realize that the brain is not speaking with a mouth. You do not hear its voice, only its thoughts.

You hear the scraping of metal feet coming from the stairwell above and behind you. Several giant spider droids climb downstairs, looking at you. From a back room come five monks in dark hooded robes. One of them giggles insanely as they draw near you. They stand with folded arms.

"My name is K'vin," the brain says to you. "You are probably wondering why I herded you here, oh bounty hunter."

"You herded me?" you ask. "I thought I came of my own accord."

"I herded you," the brain of K'vin says. "Do you know where you are?"

"I've heard that Jabba the Hutt built his palace in an old B'omarr monastery. Is this one of their monasteries?" This thought terrifies you. The B'omarr were a secretive sect, and though you know little about them, you've heard dark rumors about their vicious practices.

"No," K'vin says. "The B'omarr are a splinter group that does not follow the true path to enlightenment."

"And you know all about the true path?" you add.

"Indeed," K'vin answers. "In an effort to make the way easy, we of the Most Perfect Order of K'vin choose to shed our bodies so that we may contemplate the cosmos. The time has come for me to shed my flesh completely. I can see some of the future, and I know many things. But my mind cannot roam free so long as I am bound to this jar."

"I see . . . " you say, trying to sound wise, though in reality you have no idea what he is talking about.

"No, little bounty hunter, you do not," K'vin says quite rightly, and you wonder how much he really knows. If he can *really* read your thoughts . . . then maybe he can read Han Solo's thoughts — and tell you where he is.

"You want to know if you will catch Solo," K'vin says. "The answer is, yes, if you are persistent. You may catch him, though holding him is a more difficult matter."

"You know what I'm after then," you say. "Is Han Solo near here?"

"Very close," K'vin answers. "His ship is almost directly above me. He plans to leave soon."

You look back up the stairwell. Your only exit seems to be blocked by the spider droids. Plus, one of the monks moves to prevent you from exiting. You wonder if you can get past them, so that you can go after Han Solo.

K'vin says, "I would appreciate it if you stay."

"Okay, you're all brain, and I'm all ears," you reply. "You want something from me. What is it?"

"One small act of service," K'vin says. "Break the jar that houses my brain."

Suddenly the room rings with the sound of the five monks shouting in surprise. "No, K'vin! Don't leave us! Our training is not complete! Please, no!"

"I must leave you," K'vin answers the monks. "I who have led you so far, must now show you the way. You have sought to keep me here, but in doing so you hinder my growth."

The monks shout at you, "No, don't help him, bounty hunter. We don't want him to leave!"

You ask K'vin, "Why don't you just break the glass yourself?"

"I cannot," K'vin says. "As you see, my monks refuse to assist me, and though the spider droids are under my control, they are not programmed to destroy living creatures — only to help with conversions."

You wonder. These droids with their laser scalpels seem pretty dangerous, but according to K'vin, they won't kill you — they'll just help remove your brain.

"Look, K'vin," you say. "I don't know about this. Certainly you could get someone else to break the glass that houses your brain."

"But you are a bounty hunter," K'vin says. "Cold, passionless, and cruel. That which you must do, do quickly."

If you don't help K'vin, you are afraid that the spider droids will remove your brain. On the other hand, if you try to help him, you may have to fight the monks. There are only five monks, but at least a dozen spider droids. You decide that maybe if you help K'vin, his droids will restrain the monks. Since you can't see any other way out of this, you draw a weapon.

Suddenly, there is a hiss from the stairwell behind you. "Get him!" a monk yells.

A monk leaps at you!

He hits your arm and spoils your aim. Your weapon discharges, hitting a bottle of brains, which shatters and falls to the floor.

"Get him!" the monk shouts.

Behind you, you hear laser scalpels charging up, like the sound of dozens of miniature lightsabers turned on at once. The spider droids move to your side, weapons in hand.

From the folds of their robes, the monks also produce laser scalpels, and wave them threateningly.

You raise your weapon and aim at K'vin's brain. It's a Corellian standoff.

"Stay back," you warn the monks.

"Shoot me," K'vin says. "Shoot me, and the monks will not retaliate. I forbid them."

You are afraid to lie or bluff your way out of this, since K'vin can read your mind. You also don't trust the monks to obey K'vin.

You have two options. You can shoot K'vin, and hope that the monks don't retaliate. Or you can shoot the spider droids and leave K'vin and his followers alive.

Choose your action now, and then proceed.

To shoot K'vin: You pull the trigger, destroying the great case where his brain is housed. As you do, three monks charge to retaliate, scalpels swinging. The others hold back. Choose your weapon. Add your weaponry# to your weapon's close-range# +1 for your confront#. Roll the 12-dice.

> If your confront# is equal to or more than your roll#, add the difference to your MP total. The monk is now ready to have his brain encased with the others. Proceed to fight the next monk, until all three monks are neutralized. If you defeat all three monks without using a new confront#, add 33 MP to your MP total.

If your confront# is lower than your roll#, subtract the difference from your MP total. Add +3 to your confront# for your new confront#.

If your new confront# is equal to or more than your roll#, you may proceed to fight the next monk, until all three monks are neutralized.

If your new confront# is lower than your roll#, subtract the difference from your MP total and continue this confront with your new confront# until you have defeated all three monks.

To fight the spider droids: Only two spider droids charge, scalpels swinging. The others are held back by the monks. Choose your weapon. Add your weaponry# to your weapon's close-range# +5 for your confront#. Roll the 12-dice.

If your confront# is equal to or more than your roll#, add the difference to your MP total. That droid will never swing a laser scalpel again. Proceed to fight the second droid. Once you defeat both droids, add 20MP to your MP total.

If your confront# is lower than you roll#, subtract the difference from your MP total and repeat this confront until you have defeated the first spider droid. Once you defeat the first spider droid, you must fight the second, using the same confront equation.

You climb back up the stairs of the monastery and find a door at the back of the chapel. You had not seen it before. This door also is shut and locked, rusted with age. You know that Solo's ship is not far off, on the other side of this door, so you can't blast the door open. You must open it quietly.

You can either use Power to open the lock, use your laser scalpel to open the lock, or kick open the door.

To open the lock (using Power)*: Choose your Object Movement Power. Your skill# + your Power's low-resist# + your Power# is your confront#. Roll the 6-dice to open the lock.

If your confront# is equal to or more than your roll#, add the difference to your MP total. The door swings open easily. You may now proceed.

If your confront# is lower than your roll#, subtract the difference from your MP total. Repeat this confront until you have opened the door, and then proceed.

*Note: This counts as one of two Power uses you are allowed on this Mission.

To open the lock using the laser scalpel: Add your skill# + weaponry# + your weapon's short-range#. This is your confront#. Roll the 6-dice to open the door silently.

If your confront# is equal to or more than your roll#, add the difference to your MP total. The door silently swings open.

If your confront# is lower than your roll#, subtract the difference from your MP total. Repeat this confront using the same confront# until you have opened the door, and then proceed.

To kick open the door: Your strength# +2 is your confront#. Roll the 6-dice to open the door.

If your confront# is equal to or more than your roll#, add the difference to your MP total. The door swings open.

If your confront# is lower than your roll#, subtract the difference from your MP total. Repeat this confront using the same confront# until you have opened the door.

You break the lock and the door falls inward. A huge pile of sand pushes through, falling on you.

As you thrash about in the sand, your movement attracts a young dune worm, a small one (only ten feet long). It is the color of sand, and has enormous crystalline teeth and small beady eyes.

Since you are still trying to be quiet, you can seek to evade the worm, you can fight the dune worm with your fists, or you can fight the worm with your laser scalpel.

To evade the dune worm: You must motion in circles with your fist, hypnotizing the worm briefly, as you step back into the chapel. Add your skill#, your strength#, and your charm# for your confront#. Roll the 12-dice.

If your confront# is equal to or more than your roll#, add 10 MP to your MP total. This is one charmed worm. It is momentarily dazed, and when you retreat into the chapel it slithers after you. When it is no longer blocking your path, you continue to make circular motions for a moment, putting the worm to sleep. You then quietly proceed.

If your confront# is lower than your roll#, subtract the difference from your MP total. Add +3 to your confront# to get your new confront#.

> *If your new confront# is equal to or more than your roll#,* you have charmed the worm and can quietly proceed.

> *If your new confront# is lower than your roll#,* your charms have not worked. You must fight the worm with your fists or with your laser scalpel (below).

To combat the dune worm with your fists: Add your strength# to your skill# +1 for your confront#. Roll the 12-dice to punch out the dune worm.

> *If your confront# is equal to or more than your roll#,* add 11 MP to your MP total. It was a knockout punch. The dune worm even lost a few teeth. That will teach it to mess with a bounty hunter!

> *If your confront# is lower than your roll#,* subtract the difference from your MP total. Add +2 to your confront# to get your new confront#.

> > *If your new confront# is equal to or more than your roll#,* you have punched out the worm, and can move forward.

> > *If your new confront# is lower than your roll#,* subtract the difference from your MP total and repeat this confront until you have defeated the worm.

To combat the dune worm with your laser scalpel: Add your weaponry# to your weapon's close-range# +3 for your confront#. Roll the 12-dice.

> *If your confront# is equal to or more than your roll#,* add 9 MP to your MP total. A good solid slice like that always makes a young dune worm slither home to its mother. Just hope that *she* doesn't come after you!

> *If your confront# is lower than your roll#,* subtract the difference from your MP total. Add +2 to your confront# for your new confront#.

>> *If your new confront# is equal to or more than your roll#,* you have gotten rid of the worm. Proceed.

>> *If your new confront# is lower than your roll#,* subtract the difference from your MP total and repeat this confront until you have defeated the worm.

Once you have defeated the dune worm, add 15MP to your MP total.

You crawl up over the dune and look down into the sandy courtyard. The wind is still blowing hard, though it seems to have lightened up a little.

Han Solo's ship is there, and next to it is a small sand crawler, perhaps the only vehicle shielded enough to withstand the storm.

The lights of the landing bay are on beneath the *Millennium Falcon*, and the hatch is open.

A Gamorrean guard stands at the bottom of the hatch,

wielding a huge, double-headed axe. These guards are notoriously stupid. This one would have to be, to stand outside in a sandstorm.

The presence of the guard means that Jabba's henchmen are already here at the site. Perhaps they've come to collect Solo's payoff. Maybe they've already killed him.

You pull out your communicator and call the others, telling them that you have located Solo's ship inside an old B'omarr monastery. You warn them that Jabba might already be here. The communicator only gives off hissing static. You doubt that the others have heard you.

But you remember B'omarr's warning: Solo is about to leave. That must mean he's still alive.

You want to get closer to the ship, to learn what is happening. When the Gamorrean guard turns his back, you run swiftly over the sand.

Just as you near the hatch of the *Millennium Falcon*, the Gamorrean spots you from the corner of his eye and whirls, holding his huge war axe high.

"Whadda ya want?" he growls, his green snout wrinkling around his piglike tusks.

"Jabba sent me," you say. "To make certain that you are keeping an adequate guard."

"Really?" the Gamorrean asks.

"That's right," you say. "And for your vigilance, I'm going to recommend you for a promotion."

The Gamorrean's brow wrinkles in concentration, and his beady eyes dart back and forth. "Promotion?" he asks. "But I'm *already* chief of security!"

He frowns, and suddenly shakes with rage. "Hey, I don't believe you!" the guard says.

To get past the guard, you can either put him to sleep with Power, you can lie (with or without Power), or you can fight him.

To put the guard to sleep (using Power)*: Choose your Sleep Power. Your stealth# + your Power# + your Power's low-resist# is your confront#. Roll the 6-dice.

> If your confront# is equal to or more than your roll#, add 10 MP to your MP total. The guard won't wake up until sometime tomorrow.

> If your confront# is lower than your roll#, subtract the difference from your MP total. It didn't work. The guard is still mad, and you must either lie to him or fight him (below).

*Note: This counts as one of two Power uses you are allowed on this Mission.

To lie to the guard (using Power)*: You say, "Ah, but Jabba is going to make a new post: Supreme Pumbah of Security. And only a Gamorrean of your discerning nature could possibly fill such a position." Use your Persuasion Power. Your charm# + your Power# + your Power's low-resist# is your confront#. Roll the 6-dice.

> If your confront# is equal to or more than your roll#, add 7MP to your MP total. The guard thanks you gratefully for recommending him for a promotion and lets you pass. He will be your friend for life.

If your confront# is lower than your roll#, subtract the difference from your MP total. The guard doesn't believe you. He raises his axe to swing. You must fight (below).

*Note: This counts as one of two Power uses you are allowed on this Mission.

To lie to the guard (without Power): You say, "Ah, but Jabba is going to make a new post. That of Supreme Pumbah of Security. And only a Gamorrean of your discerning nature could possibly fill such a position." Your charm# +1 is your confront#. Roll the 6-dice.

If your confront# is equal to or more than your roll#, add 9MP to your MP total. The guard grovels at your feet, begging you not to forget to recommend him for the promotion. Then he lets you pass.

If your confront# is lower than your roll#, subtract the difference from your MP total. The guard doesn't believe you, and raises his axe to swing. You must fight (below).

To fight the Gamorrean guard: You grab his weapon with one hand and choke him with the other. Your strength# + your skill# + your stealth# +1 is your confront#. Roll the 12-dice to fight the guard.

If your confront# is equal to or more than your roll#, add 7MP to your MP total. You have defeated the guard.

If your confront# is lower than your roll#, subtract the difference from your MP total. Add +1 to your confront# for your new confront#.

If your new confront# is equal to or more than your roll#, add the difference to your MP total. The guard is now out of your way.

If your new confront# is lower than your roll#, subtract the difference from your MP total and repeat this confront until you have defeated the guard.

With the guard out of the way, you begin to creep aboard the *Millennium Falcon.*

As you step halfway up the gangplank, you hear voices. You must sneak onto the ship.

To sneak onto the ship: Your stealth# +2 is your confront#. Roll the 6-dice to sneak onboard.

If your confront# is equal to or more than your roll#, add the difference to your MP total. You have slipped aboard the ship quietly.

If your confront# is lower than your roll#, you have made a slight noise. Subtract 4MP from your MP total and try again, until you gain entry onto the ship.

You pass through the hallways, and notice an open repair hatch. It looks as if Solo has been trying to fix a hyperdrive link. The link is badly scored with burn marks and probably isn't any good. Solo won't be able to take off if he can't make it into hyperspace, so you reach down and pull out the hyperdrive link, laughing grimly to yourself.

As you do, you hear someone talking in the sleeping

bay. You stick your head into the access hall that leads to the pilots' cabin. The pilots' seats are empty. But you notice that in the pilots' module, some security monitors are showing pictures of the interior of the ship. Everything you've done so far has been caught on camera.

You wave to the camera, then creep closer to the pilot's seat to the monitor that shows what is happening in the sleeping bay.

In the sleeping bay, you see two droids. A golden protocol droid and a little R2 astromech unit. A woman sits in the shadows behind them, head down, as if in thought.

You also see two creatures, creatures who aren't much more handsome than the Gamorrean was outside. One of them looks like some Trandoshan cloning experiment gone awry. His body is badly scarred. The other has pointed ears and greenish skin.

On the table between them is a long brown creature that looks like a worm or a slug. It has an enormous mouth and rich yellow eyes. A young Hutt. Some small animal squirms in the Hutt's paws.

"Oh, Princess Leia, I can't abide this baby Hutt and its filthy habits," the golden droid says. "I certainly hope that Master Solo and Master Luke get back soon."

The little R2 unit gives an electronic beep of agreement.

"You're lucky that Jabba feels generous," one thug grumbles — the Trandoshan who is all muscle and scar tissue.

"Generous?" the diplomatic droid echoes. "He wants his nephew back — *and* ten thousand credits? That's not generous! It's extortion!"

"Ha, ha, ha," the little Hutt laughs. "You doubt my Ur-Damo's generosity? Jabba will have your metal parts melted down into sewer pipes for that."

"Please, Grubba," the golden droid scolds the Hutt, "you should be grateful that we saved you! Imagine, being held for ransom by a rival crime lord! You should thank Master Solo."

"I'm gonna tell my Ur-Damo that *you* kidnapped me," Grubba says. "I'll help him torture a confession from you!"

The thugs all laugh at Grubba's jokes, while the golden droid rattles with fright.

"Jabba and the others should be here any minute," Leia says, trying to calm the protocol droid. You see that she is wearing wristbands and shackles. She, too, is a prisoner here.

"Yeah, then we'll see what he decides to do with you all," the green guard says.

At the news, you become nervous. If Jabba and his goons come into the ship, you're sure to be caught. Taking on Han Solo and his Rebel friends would be hard enough, but you can't fight Jabba's whole criminal empire.

You're alone. The other bounty hunters are far away. Even if they were to come now, your party wouldn't be able to fight both Solo's group and Jabba's cohorts.

As you realize this, you come up with a daring plan.

You had hoped that Solo would pay Jabba off in coin. That way you could steal the money.

But Jabba wants Grubba, and is offering a reward.

Maybe he'd pay the reward to you?

Or maybe he'd trade Han for the child?

Or maybe, if the child was taken, Han and Jabba would fight it out.

In any case, if you can't get Solo now, having the Hutt will ensure that you get him later. . . .

You go to take the child. You can either take Grubba by lying without Power, by lying with Power, by putting the guards to sleep with Power, or by fighting the guards.

To lie (without Power): You tell the guards that Jabba has sent you as a courier to pick up the child, and that the guards are to hold Leia, the droids, and the ship until further notice. Your charm# +5 is your confront#. Roll the 12-dice to deceive the guards.

> *If your confront # is equal to or more than your roll#,* add 10 MP to your MP total. The guards believe you, and give you custody of Grubba the Hutt.

> *If your confront# is lower than your roll#,* subtract the difference from your MP total. The guards don't believe you, and you must fight them (below).

To lie (using Power)*: You tell the guards that Jabba has sent you as a courier to pick up the child, and that the guards are to hold the droids, Leia, and the ship until further notice. Choose your Persuasion Power or your Deception Power. Your charm# + your Power's medium-resist# + your Power# is your confront#. Roll the 6-dice to deceive the guards.

> *If your confront# is equal to or more than your roll number,* add 6 MP to your MP total. The guards give you Grubba the Hutt.

If your confront# is lower than your roll#, subtract the difference from your MP total. The guards don't believe you. "Shoot him," the leader shouts. You must fight (below).

*Note: This counts as one of two Power uses you are allowed on this Mission.

To put the guards to sleep (with Power)*: Choose your Sleep Power. Your stealth# + your Power# + your Power's medium-resist# is your confront#. Roll the 12-dice.

If your confront# is equal to or more than your roll#, add 7 MP to your MP total. The guards drop in their chairs, snoring loudly.

If your confront# is lower than your roll#, subtract the difference from your MP total. It didn't work. The guards are still awake, and you must fight (below).

*Note: This counts as one of two Power uses you are allowed on this Mission.

To fight: Choose your weapon. Add your weaponry# to your weapon's close-range# for your confront#. Roll the 6-dice to combat the first guard.

If your confront# is equal to or more than your roll#, add the difference to your MP total, and proceed to combat the second guard, using the same confront equation.

If your confront# is lower than your roll#, subtract the difference from your MP total. Add +2 to your confront# for your new confront#.

> *If your new confront# is equal to or more than your roll#,* you have defeated the first guard. Add 1 MP to your MP total. Now use your new confront# to defeat the second guard. When you have defeated the second guard, you may proceed.

> *If your new confront# is lower than your roll#,* subtract the difference from your MP total and repeat this confront until you have defeated both guards.

Once you defeat the guards, add 25 MP to your total (50 MP for Advanced Level players).

You grab the young Hutt and leave the ship. Grubba squirms in your arms, so you hold on tight. The sand is ripping across the desert and bites you like the teeth of a dune worm. You run quickly through the gates of the old B'omarr fortress. The child wriggles in your arms like a fish, and is twice as slimy.

"Let go of me, you goon!" Grubba hollers. "You're not any better than those rotten Rebels."

He bites you on the arm. At first you just think it's the sand biting your flesh.

"Ew, you taste dirty," Grubba says.

"Knock it off, you brat," you say.

"You'll be even dirtier once my Ur-Damo plants your miserable carcass in the ground," Grubba shouts.

"Quiet," you say, "or I'll stuff you in my saddlebag."

The young Hutt glares at you with petulant rage, and quiets down.

As you round the corner of the fortress, you hear the engines of a large sand crawler drawing near. Its heavy treads clank over the ground, and the sand beneath your feet shifts and rumbles.

In the darkness of the storm, you rush to your dewback. You can't easily direct the creature and hold Grubba at the same time, so as the child curses you, you stuff him in your saddlebag and fasten it closed.

Grubba shouts and wriggles.

You don't even try to use your communicator. Instead, you ride like mad with your back to the wind, hoping only to escape.

Every moment, you imagine that you hear the sound of blasters or that you can feel something more than sand ripping through your back.

Fortunately, you made your trip on the dewback. If you had brought a metal vehicle, perhaps Jabba's sand crawler would have been able to detect the metal or the electronics. As it is, you *might* be able to make it.

You use the few landmarks that you can locate to guide yourself on the journey. You call out to your party over the communicator from time to time, but you still cannot hear anything but static in return.

Finally, you reach the place where you fought the Sand People.

There, you see something huge. Amid the swirling

clouds of sand, two horned beasts are feeding on the carrion of the dead bantha.

Since they are already feeding, you hope they won't attack you.

But krayt dragons like their food alive.

The monsters rush with their claws extended, roaring
above the shriek of the wind.

You must either evade the dragons or fight them.

To evade the dragons: You must turn your dewback
around and race away into the blinding storm. You do this by
kicking the creature hard and shouting for it to hurry. Your
charm# + your stealth# + the dewback's speed# + the dewback's stealth# is your confront#. Roll the 12-dice to evade the
dragons.

> *If your confront# is equal to or more than your roll#,* add
> 20 MP to your MP total. The dragons quickly lose sight
> of you in the blinding sandstorm. You may proceed.

> *If your confront# is lower than your roll#,* subtract the dif-
> ference from your MP total. The dragons are not so
> easily evaded, and attack. You must fight (below).

To fight the dragons: Add your weaponry# to your
weapon's far-range# for your confront#. Roll the 6-dice to combat the first dragon.

> *If your confront# is equal to or more than your roll#,* add
> 10 MP to your MP total. Your shot was a perfect hit.
> The dragon figures that even though it's still hungry,
> maybe a nice Jawa will do instead of you. It leaves. Pro-

ceed to combat the second dragon, using the same confront equation. Once you have defeated the second dragon, add 7 MP to your MP total and proceed.

If your confront# is lower than your roll#, subtract the difference from your MP total and repeat this confront until you defeat both dragons.

The dragons are gone, yet from time to time as you battle your way across the sands, you hear them roaring. They are so big and fierce, you fear that if they make a concerted attack, you'll just be another meal. Worse, with all that roaring, they might attract friends.

You worm your way back and forth through the sands for awhile, lost.

Suddenly, you hear a weak voice on your communicator!

"We've got your locator coming in strong! What's your report? Was that Solo's ship?"

"Affirmative," you reply.

There is a long silence. The voice on the communicator says, "Don't tell me he got away!"

"For now," you reply. "But I know how to get him back." You pat the saddlebag, where Grubba the Hutt has gone limp.

From the bag, Grubba roars. "You wait until Jabba finds out what you've done!"

The voice on the communicator tells you, "All right. Angle thirty degrees to your right. We'll guide you on in."

Hot, sandy, and weary to the bone, you reach the biosphere with the nasty child still shouting curses from inside the saddlebag.

This has been a difficult Mission. You have not captured Solo, but you have captured something that Solo desperately needs. Award yourself 110 MP (140 for Advanced Level players).

THE AFTER-MISSION

Aboard the *Millennium Falcon*, Han Solo was backed against a wall. A good dozen of Jabba's Gamorrean henchmen were aboard ship, and Solo and his friends were weaponless.

The Gamorreans had Chewbacca cornered, and another held Leia back. Luke, too, was shoved against a far wall.

At that moment, Han suspected that the only ones who would get out of this alive were the droids. And working as slaves for Jabba would hardly be much better than a quick termination.

Bib Fortuna, Jabba's majordomo, was outraged to find that the young Grubba had been kidnapped again. Jabba wasn't here. The crime lord who had kidnapped young Grubba in the first place, a whiphid named "Black Tongue," had just been captured. Jabba was now teaching the whiphid a serious lesson of his own devising.

So he had sent Bib Fortuna to retrieve his beloved Ur-Damin.

"Death for you, Han Solo, for this," Bib Fortuna hissed, his Twi'lek head tail's lashing. He put a long blue finger against Han's jugular vein, and poked with a pointed nail until a drop of blood flowed.

"But it's not my fault!" Han objected. Certainly Bib Fortuna knew that. He'd seen the images captured by the ship's security system. If anyone was to blame for losing the child, it was Jabba's own guards.

"Still, Jabba's anger must be assuaged. . . . " Bib Fortuna hissed. To his guards, he said, "Take them now."

"Wait," Luke Skywalker said, looking earnestly into Bib Fortuna's red eyes. "Jabba is not angry with Han, nor will he be." Desperately, Luke hoped the Force would work. He had seen Obi-Wan Kenobi use the Force to persuade others, but Luke had to persuade so many of these guards at once.

Slowly, as if in a daze, Bib Fortuna cocked his head as if listening to distant music, and said, "Jabba . . . will not be angry."

"Han and Jabba are old friends," Luke said.

"Old friends," Bib Fortuna repeated. The Force was working!

"You should let Han and his friends go, so that they may quickly pursue the men who stole Jabba's Ur-Damin. Only this course of action will please Jabba."

Luke stared hard at Bib Fortuna, and after a moment, the Twi'lek turned away, his head tail going limp as it relaxed. "Let them go. Let them all go," Bib Fortuna ordered the Gamorrean guards. "Quickly!"

"You are wise," Luke said, "and your master will praise you."

In their biosphere, the bounty hunters gathered around the young Grubba.

"You are all dead for this!" Grubba shouted. He pointed a stubby finger at each bounty hunter in turn. "You! You! And you!"

"I don't think so," Dengar said. "Jabba knows what we're fishing for. And a little worm of a Hutt like you is the perfect bait."

Eron had been listening over the biosphere's communicators. "The news is all over the air. Jabba is doubling the reward for the return of Grubba. Apparently he feels that the family honor has been doubly spotted."

Her glance passed over to Udin.

"I'm not completely sure I like this idea," Udin said. "How do we know Han Solo will come for the child?"

"Because," Eron Stonefield said, "at the same time that he increased the reward for young Grubba, he also increased the bounty on Han Solo. Now, if Han wants to pay off his death price, he'll be much more desperate to get the kid back."

Outside, the storm was quieting. With the rising of the suns, the low-lying Dune Sea would heat up again, and the storms would abate for another sizzling day.

"Okay," young Grubba groaned. "I'll come with you, as long as you take me someplace fun. And if Jabba pays a reward for me, I get half."

Udin the Kubaz wrinkled his short trunk, and the translator said, "Do you like bugs?"

"I like to pull their legs off, and then eat them," Grubba said.

"On my world," Udin said, "the bugs are big enough to pull the legs off *you*, before they eat *you*."

"Ha, ha, ha," Grubba laughed. "Then I'm glad I don't have legs."

"The bugs there like to eat worms, too," Udin replied. After a long moment of thought he added, "I'll leave a few clues for Han with one of my hive-mates at Mos Eisley. Then we'll lead Han into our trap. He'll get a warm reception on my home world — Kubindi. Once he comes there, I promise, he will never return. . . . "

NEXT MISSION: THE SEARCH FOR GRUBBA THE HUTT